Jack's Best Boots

Jack's Best Boots

Boots

AND OTHER STORIES OF LONG AGO
Compiled by the Editors
of
Highlights for Children

BOYDS MILLS PRESS

Compilation copyright © 1993 by Boyds Mills Press, Inc.
Contents copyright by Highlights for Children, Inc.
All rights reserved

Published by Boyds Mills Press, Inc.
A Highlights Company
815 Church Street
Honesdale, Pennsylvania 18431
Printed in the United States of America

Publisher Cataloging-in-Publication Data
Main entry under title :
    Jack's best boots : and other stories of long ago / compiled by the
editors of Highlights for Children.—1st ed.
[96]p. : cm.
Stories originally published in *Highlights for Children*.
Summary: A collection of historical fiction for children.
ISBN 1-56397-266-2
1. Children's stories. I. Highlights for Children. II. Title.
    [F]   1993   CIP
The Library of Congress Catalog Card Number :93-70409

First edition, 1993
Book designed by Tim Gillner
The text of this book is set in 12-point Garamond.
Distributed by St. Martin's Press

Highlights is a registered trademark of Highlights for Children, Inc.

CONTENTS

Jack's Best Boots

By Ann Bixby Herold

It was a long walk from Albany, New York, to Valley Forge, Pennsylvania. Debby thought they would never get there.

Each night, as she and her mother hunted for a place to sleep, she asked, "Are we nearly there, Ma?" Each night her mother wearily shook her head. After hours of trudging over slush-covered roads, she was too tired to talk.

At first, each mile had been an adventure. It was

early spring in 1778 and they were heading south to a family reunion. Debby's father, John Ford, and her brother, Jack, were both serving in the Continental Army under General Washington. The army had been encamped at Valley Forge since December.

"This is like a rescue mission," Debby thought.

She and her mother walked wrapped in blankets, to keep warm. In their backpacks they carried food and clothing for the menfolk. Jack's best boots hung around Debby's neck. A present from his cousin Robert, who had outgrown them, the fine leather boots were Jack's pride and joy. They had been made by the best boot maker in Albany. Robert's father was a rich merchant, not a poor farmer like John Ford.

"Keep them polished until I return, Deb," Jack had said when he left.

"Why don't you take them with you?" she asked.

"March through snow and mud in my best boots?" Jack asked with horror. "Besides, they're too big. My old ones will do."

As snow lay deep around their snug little farmhouse, news arrived in Albany of the desperate state of the troops at Valley Forge.

"It's not right they should suffer so," said Mrs. Ford.

"We're suffering, too, Ma," Debby reminded her. "We've had no milk since we sold the cow."

"We're living in luxury compared to the soldiers,

Debby. To think they've gone the winter through without enough food or clothing!"

The letter that started them on their journey had arrived one bitter winter day while they were chopping wood.

It was from Jack, and it was the first letter they had received in months. Except for the line *I could do with my best boots right now, Deb,* it was so cheery that Mrs. Ford was suspicious. "Your father must have told him not to make me worry. I should never have let him go. He's only twelve." She wiped her eyes on her apron.

"He's not the only drummer boy there," said Debby. "There's his friend Alexander Milliner. Jack says here that Alexander's mother works as a laundress at the camp. You could do the same, Ma. Why don't you go to Valley Forge?"

It was a crazy idea. But knowing that another drummer boy had his mother with him was all Mrs. Ford needed to spur her on. "I'll need money. We'll sell the chickens and the ducks. With the neighbors' help, you can mind the house."

Debby was only nine, but she had ideas of her own. "I'm going, too, Ma. I have to take Jack his best boots."

That was three weeks ago. Now, after a week on the road, the snow had disappeared. Their pace increased with their stamina. Nightfall was the low point of the day.

Sometimes they were lucky. They'd knock at a farmhouse door and be welcomed at the family supper table. Other times they were given bread and a corner of the barn. Only twice were they turned away. Once they shivered all night under a bridge. The other time they buried themselves deep in a damp haystack. When their money ran out, they did chores in return for a meal and a place to sleep. More than once they were offered good money for Jack's boots, which hung like heavy weights around Debby's neck. But she refused to sell them.

The weather grew steadily warmer. On sunny days they sang as they walked. On the last leg of their long journey they met a fellow New Yorker, a soldier on his way home on furlough. "Your brother is the best drummer boy at Valley Forge," he told Debby.

Twenty miles from the camp they caught up with a convoy of wagons loaded with supplies and pulled by oxen. They rode the rest of the way, sitting on sacks of potatoes. When they entered the camp, Debby heard a drum. The oxen were moving too slowly for her. She slid to the ground and raced ahead, Jack's boots swinging from one hand.

She came to a field. Soldiers in mismatched uniforms were marching up and down. The drummer boy tapping to the beat wasn't Jack. But when she asked him about her brother, he pointed toward some huts.

"Jack? Jack?" she called as she ran toward them. A tall boy came out of a hut. "Jack!" Debby cried. "You've *grown*."

"Deb?" He gaped at her. "What are you doing here?"

"I've brought your best boots," she said, laughing. "And Ma has come to wash your clothes. Where's Pa?"

"On guard duty." He shook his head in disbelief. "You brought my boots?"

Jack's feet were bound in sacking and stuffed into boots several sizes too large. He kicked them off.

Debby bit her lip. "What if they don't fit anymore?"

"They were too big, remember?" With a sigh of pleasure, Jack pulled on his boots. They were just right.

The Ragman's Music

By Judith Logan Lehne

"Rags! Rags!"

The tired but strangely musical words bumped along the cobblestone street.

"Rags! Rags!" The old man sang to the clip-clop rhythm of his horse's hoofs.

Scrunched in a far corner of her papa's dry goods store, Anna heard the ragman's call. She rested an old flute on her knees and shivered a little. Would her mother want her to carry the fabric scraps to the

ragman again? She hoped not. She scrunched farther into the corner and whispered into her cotton
dress, "He smells like his horse! And his scraggly
beard sticks out like wires."

"Rags! Rags!" The call was nearer. Soon the ragman would stop outside Papa's store.

Anna put the flute to her lips and whistle-blew
into it, just as Grandma had shown her. Only flat
squeaks and shrills escaped from the instrument.
Anna frowned at the tarnished flute and stood up.
"Ugly flutes can't make pretty songs," she said.
"Who needs this old thing?"

"Rags! Rags!" The ragman's sing-song voice gave
Anna an idea. She found Mother behind the counter
measuring Mrs. Finnegan's fabric.

"Mother, do you have anything for the ragman
today?" she asked.

Mother pulled fabric pieces from a large crate and
heaped them into Anna's arms. Then she opened a
tin and scooped out some taffy. "Our ragman has a
sweet tooth," she said. She put the candy on top of
the pile in Anna's arms and smiled. Anna slid the
flute under the rags and ran to the street.

The ragman was perched on the wooden plank
that stretched across his shabby cart. His patched
pants bagged around his scuffed boots. Anna noticed
a large hole in the bottom of one boot. He pulled
the reins. "Whoa-a," he murmured, and his dappled
gray horse pawed at the ground. The cart creaked

as the ragman climbed down.

"Ah, Anna. Such rich rags," he said, fingering the fabric with peculiar tenderness. His cart was already quite full. The silk and brocade scraps from Papa's store looked out of place scattered over the mound of tattered rags.

"Thank your kind mama for the sweets," he said, hoisting himself back into the cart and grasping the reins in his leathery hands.

"Wait!" Anna shouted. "Here." She stood on her tiptoes and handed him the flute. His brown eyes clouded slightly, then warmed.

"You can keep it. Or sell it," Anna said. "Only ugly music comes from an old flute."

"There's no *ugly* music, my child," the ragman said. "You'll see." There was a faraway look in his eyes. As she watched the ragman and her flute disappear around the corner, Anna felt an odd lump in her throat.

"Dumb old flute," she sighed.

Weeks passed, and the ragman didn't come. Anna waited for his call every day. The fishman came, and the vegetable man, and the iceman, but not the ragman. Anna tried to forget about the flute.

She was cutting paper dolls when she heard it: an enchanting melody, rich and lively, floating through the open window. Anna dropped her scissors and peered out at the street. The music—flute music— came nearer and then stopped.

"Rags! Rags!" The ragman's voice was different. Not so tired. Anna ran to the scrap crate, grabbed an armful of fabric, and hurried to the old man's cart.

"My flute!" she cried. "You made beautiful music with my old flute!"

The ragman's eyes twinkled. "Come here, my dear," he said.

"His voice is *kind,*" thought Anna. "Why was I so afraid of him before?"

The ragman took Anna's hand and walked to the back of the cart. Shaking a finger at the rags, he asked, "What do you see here, Anna?"

"Old rags," Anna said.

"Can you see a rug?" he asked. "Or a doll?"

"Of course not!" Anna replied.

"Watch, child," he told her.

The ragman crumpled a faded tan cloth into his fist. He found another tan piece and draped it over the crumpled rag. He rolled fabric into smooth ropes. He ripped rags into strips, tying them here and there. He was stooped over the back of the cart as he worked.

"Find me some satin from your mama's scraps," he said, "and a bit of gingham." His bent, brown fingers worked quickly.

He was smiling all over when he completed his task and held up the doll for Anna.

"Just old rags, Anna?"

Unblinking, Anna held the doll in one hand,

charmed by the blue satin dress gathered at the waist with a ribbon. A sweet gingham scarf was tied under the chin of the faceless doll.

Opening Anna's other hand, the ragman wrapped her fingers around the flute.

"You see, my dear," the ragman said, "tarnish and tatters don't matter. What's inside, that's the thing."

Before Anna could speak, the ragman climbed onto his perch and urged his horse past the store. His voice echoed in her ears, "Rags! Rags!"

Anna kissed the doll, then raised the flute to her lips. "Yes," she said. "*That's* the thing."

The Long Ride

By R. E. Richards

David Jay arose and stumbled bleary-eyed to the long, wooden-plank breakfast table. A steaming plate of fried eggs was waiting for him. He gobbled down his breakfast, snatched up a water flask and packet of dried beef jerky, and rushed outside.

In the dim morning light David could just barely make out the lanky form of Mr. Thompson, the station keeper. Mr. Thompson stood alongside the log station house, holding the reins of a horse.

In the distance came the thunder of hoofbeats as a rider approached at full gallop. The dusty, buckskinned rider, a young man of about nineteen, pulled his horse up alongside Mr. Thompson. The rider sprang from the saddle, pulled leather mail pouches from the back of his horse, and slipped them over the saddle of the horse that Mr. Thompson was holding.

In an instant David leaped into the saddle of the fresh horse and was off at full speed. The sun was just peeking above the edge of the Nebraska plains.

David began his daily race against time. He was a Pony Express rider. The Pony Express was a cross-country mail company. Its riders carried pouches of mail between St. Joseph, Missouri, and Sacramento, California. For months David had carried the mail back and forth across the Nebraska territory in this "relay race" on horseback.

After an hour's ride David approached the first swing station. Swing stations were spaced about fifteen miles apart along the Pony Express route. At the station, riders could exchange tired horses for fresh ones. David dismounted and handed the reins of his sweating, exhausted horse to the station keeper, who put the mail onto a new horse. Moments later, David was again flying along the trail.

Late in the day, David pulled up to the Fort Kearny express station, sore and tired from his long ride. Karl, the station keeper, rushed out to meet him.

"David, we've got a problem," explained Karl. "Charlie was attacked by bandits and wounded. I don't have a rider to take the mail to Cold Springs."

David knew that, above all else, the mail must get through.

"I'll make the trip," he replied quickly.

Although he dreaded riding another eighty miles on the trail, David was glad to get a chance to go to Cold Springs. Old Hank Torrens was the Cold Springs station keeper. Hank had been a good friend of David's family. It was Hank who had taught David to ride.

David stayed in Fort Kearny only long enough to eat a hot meal and catch his breath. Back in the saddle, he rode westward toward the setting sun.

Darkness came soon and David had to slow his pace. But the moon was full, and it was fairly easy to follow the trail.

By the time David arrived at the fifth and last relay station, his body ached from seventeen hours in the saddle. He longed to rest, but he knew that if he stopped even for a short while, he would never be able to get up and finish the ride.

For miles, David rode on through the darkness. Suddenly, he heard the sound of hoofbeats close behind. Mail bandits! David dug his spurs into the horse's sides. The horse responded with a burst of speed. His mount, a thin boy and twenty pounds of mail, was the lighter load. The sound of riders grew fainter and fainter.

Just about the time David had put a safe cushion of distance between himself and the bandits, his horse stepped into a hole, stumbled, and fell. David was pitched headlong onto the trail. Shaken but unhurt, he ran back to remount and continue his ride. The horse had gotten to its feet but was limping badly. David's heart sank when he realized the injury was too serious for the horse to be ridden.

He led the crippled horse off the trail, listening all the while for hoofbeats. But the cool night air was still and silent. He slid the mail pouches off the horse's back and slung them over his own shoulders. He would come back later for the horse.

Back on the trail, David ran in the direction of Cold Springs with the precious pouches bouncing against his chest. On and on he went. The mail pouches felt like thousand-pound weights dragging him to the ground.

His last ounce of strength was gone, but David's legs kept moving—driven by the desire to complete his mission. Finally, he could go no farther. He collapsed onto the cold ground, totally spent.

In his dazed, weary mind, David thought he was in a cabin, resting comfortably by a warm, crackling fire. But the sound of approaching hoofbeats quickly snapped him back to reality. Bandits? The rider stopped. David clutched the mail tightly, dreading what might happen next. But at the rider's gentle touch he soon relaxed. When he opened his eyes, he found himself peering into the kind, smiling face of his friend Old Hank.

••

Riders like David Jay began delivering American mail in April of 1860. The Pony Express could deliver messages 12 to 14 days faster than stagecoaches. However, the completion of a coast-to-coast telegraph system meant the Pony Express was no longer needed. On October 24, 1861, the Pony Express made its last run.

Turkey Red

By Esther L. Vogt

Anna Barkman hunched over as she plunked another fat red wheat kernel into the tin pail. She shook her thick brown braids and sighed. She was tired. It took so long!

Yet, Pa had said, "Pick only the largest, plumpest grains—those with reddish-gold color. The pale, small, soft ones you must throw aside. Next month we will begin our long journey to America, and we must take only the finest wheat for seed."

So eight-year-old Anna picked and plunked—a slow, tiresome job—to fill two buckets, one kernel at a time. For a week she had worked in the hot loft where the seed wheat was stored. Anna thought she must have picked a million kernels by now!

But her mind bubbled as she worked. It was exciting to think of leaving Caslov, in the Crimean Peninsula of southern Russia, and moving to a new land. Even though the Mennonites had a good life on the fertile steppes, they were not happy with the government and so had decided to leave. Twenty-three families were leaving with the Barkmans.

There were many things to pack. Every day Anna heard Pa sawing and hammering as he made huge boxes in which to pack their belongings.

Amid heavy woolen clothes (for winter) and an extra supply of aprons and scarves, Pa packed the two buckets of precious Turkey Red seed wheat.

"Did I pick out the kernels as you wished, Pa?" Anna asked wistfully as she watched him pack.

He squeezed her arm gently. "The best wheat in the world! You have been very patient and have done your work well. Here!" he said. He fumbled through the pockets of his homespun trousers and drew out a handful of hazelnuts. "These are for you—for all the work you did."

On May 1, 1874, the group of Mennonites left the Crimea and took a boat from Caslov across the Black Sea to Odessa. From there they rode on trains across

Europe, then they sailed for England. In Liverpool they walked up the gangplank of the steamship *City of Brooklyn* and left for America.

Six weeks later, a sailor shouted, "I see land!"

Anna clung to her father's hand as she peered over the railing toward the west. Foam crested on breakers, and the sea pounded against the sides of the ship. It didn't look like land to Anna. Instead, it seemed more like a big black cloud.

But Pa squeezed her small hand very gently. "This is America," he said.

America! Would they soon reach their new home? Anna's heart raced.

After the *City of Brooklyn* steamed into New York harbor, the dockhands began to unload the cargo. Anna watched as they carted away the wooden chest in which her precious seed wheat was stored.

Everyone was loaded down with bags and boxes for the trip to the train station. The group of 163 Mennonites boarded the train.

Early one August morning the train chugged into Peabody, Kansas. All on board were fast asleep, and no one noticed the door of the coach slide open until Jakob Wiebe shouted, "Everyone asleep?"

Blinking foggily, the people jumped up, scrambled to the door, and looked out. Kansas at last!

Peabody, a little dusty village with rough-board stores and a few shabby houses, drowsed in the hot summer sunshine. Prairie grass covered a treeless world like an endless sea.

With Jakob Wiebe as their leader, the group bought wagons and teams, and lumbered across the prairie to their new homes.

Every day the hot winds blew over the tall grass that rose and fell like angry sea waves, and little Anna Barkman grew afraid.

"Look at the high grass!" she cried. "How can our Turkey Red ever grow here?"

But Pa only smiled. After they had built shanties and dug wells, the men began to plow. In three weeks the warm September rains fell and broke the summer's heat. Soon the wheat sprouted, and by late autumn the prairies were checkered with squares of green.

When the wheat was harvested, the Barkman yield was higher than that of most of their neighbors. All the Mennonites living at Gnadenau (also called Grace Meadow Village) raised good wheat, for others had also brought along a bit of good Turkey Red seed wheat. Soon word spread across Kansas that the Mennonites had a new kind of wheat that grew well in the hot Kansas sunshine and made better flour than any other kind. It could also withstand the bitter cold winters, and the hard Turkey Red wheat made the best bread. (It was called *Turkey* because it first grew in a little valley in Turkey and *Red* because of its reddish-gold color.)

Before the Mennonites brought Turkey Red to

America, the Kansas farmers had not raised much wheat. Since then, Kansas has become known as the "wheat state" and the "breadbasket of the nation."

A long time has passed since Anna Barkman's exciting journey to America. The village of Gnadenau has disappeared and Anna Barkman is no longer alive. But Turkey Red's importance is still felt. It is the grandparent of most winter wheat grown today.

Silver Buttons

By Ann Bixby Herold

Jamie's grandmother stopped weaving and peered at him over her loom. Candlelight softened the harsh expression on her face.

"General Washington is asking us to make jackets for real soldiers," she said. "Not for boys who think they're soldiers."

"I didn't say I was a soldier, Grandmother," Jamie replied. "I only said I need a jacket as much as any soldier."

"The soldiers are fighting for us, Jamie," said his father from his seat by the fire. "They've a long winter ahead of them. Their need is greater than yours."

"But why can't Grandmother weave enough cloth for two jackets?"

"Stop your pestering!" she snapped.

A few days later the length of thick warm homespun was finished. Jamie examined the dark blue cloth when no one was around. He dared not ask if there was enough for two jackets.

"I cut out the jacket this forenoon," said his mother at supper.

Jamie waited while she passed around bowls of steaming broth.

"Did you have enough cloth, Mother?" he asked as he reached for a piece of bread.

"Are you asking if there is enough left over for you?" she replied. Her eyes twinkled.

Jamie blushed and nodded.

"There is if you promise not to grow for a while."

"I promise!" cried Jamie.

"Then make him one and that's an end to it," said his father.

At last the soldier's jacket was finished. Decorated with bone buttons from Grandmother's trinket box, it looked fine enough for General Washington.

When Jamie's jacket was finished, there was a problem.

"The wooden buttons on your old jacket are

broken or missing," said his mother. "And there's not a spare button in the house."

Jamie didn't care. The jacket was warm and comfortable.

"For now, a jacket without buttons is good enough," he said. "I'll carve my own."

But somehow, with lessons and the farm chores, there was never enough time.

One snowy, stormy afternoon Jamie was walking home from a neighboring farm. Head down against a cold wind, he rounded a bend and almost walked into a man on horseback. The rider sat hunched in the saddle, his tricorn pulled low, his cloak wrapped close about him. Jamie didn't recognize horse or rider. As he stepped aside to let them pass, the stranger hailed him.

"Hey there, lad. I fear I have lost my way. Is this the road to Philadelphia?"

Jamie eyed him uneasily. The times were dangerous. No one wanted to meet a stranger on a lonely country road.

"You took the wrong road a way back," said Jamie.

As the wind whipped the words away, the man leaned forward to hear him.

"Aye, I thought as much. Is there an inn hereabouts?" he asked. "I'm weary and chilled to the bone."

He flashed a tired smile from the depths of his cloak. Jamie's heart went out to him.

"There's no tavern for miles," Jamie replied, "but

if you follow me, I believe my family will give you shelter."

Wading ahead through the drifting snow, Jamie's heart sank further with every step. What if his parents were angry? In such times there was no telling friend from foe. Just who might this man be?

Jamie's fears were confirmed when he led the stranger into their warm kitchen. His father gave him a dark look. His mother studied the stranger nervously.

The atmosphere eased when the man took off his cloak. He appeared to be a prosperous older gentleman. Even Jamie's grandmother relaxed enough to smooth down her apron and pat her hair.

"We don't often see strangers around these parts," said Jamie's father cautiously.

"Charles Ward at your service, sir," the stranger said. He smiled and bowed. "I am on my way to Philadelphia. I was lost and looking for an inn."

Jamie's parents exchanged glances.

"I guess we can offer you a meal," said his father.

"To be out of the weather on such a night, I would gladly bed down in your barn, if you would permit it," said Mr. Ward.

Jamie's grandmother looked shocked.

"The barn? Nay, sir! We have no spare bed, but we can offer you the settle, here by the fire," she said.

And so it was decided.

The family sat spellbound all through supper as

Mr. Ward told them about his travels. He mentioned neither the war nor politics, for which they were silently grateful.

At bedtime their guest was made comfortable by the fire. By morning the storm was over. Jamie saddled Mr. Ward's horse and brought it around to the door. Mr. Ward's offer of money was refused by Jamie's father.

"There's no price on hospitality," he said. "Jamie will set you on the right road. Good-bye to you, sir."

Jamie gazed around as he rode behind Mr. Ward. The snow sparkled in the bright sunlight. A mile from the farm he tapped Mr. Ward on the shoulder and slid to the ground.

"Take the right fork up ahead," he said. "Ride to the village of Barnbridge. Someone there will put you on the Philadelphia road."

"Thank you, Jamie," said Mr. Ward. He leaned down to shake Jamie's hand. "Tell me one thing. That's a fine new jacket you're wearing. Why does it have no buttons?"

Jamie knew better than to mention the soldier's jacket. "My mother had none to spare, but I'm going to carve my own," said Jamie.

"Well, I would give you money for buttons in payment for my night's lodging, but I know your father would be angry. Instead, take these," said Mr. Ward.

He dug into his saddlebag and handed down a small leather bag. Jamie's cold fingers fumbled as he opened it. He reached inside and brought out a handful of icy cold silver buttons. They shone like jewels in the sunlight.

"I bought them myself on my last visit to France," said Mr. Ward. He smiled down at Jamie's astonished face. "I want you to have them."

Jamie started to say that they were too fine for his jacket, but with a wave, Mr. Ward rode away.

Jamie hurried home and burst into the kitchen.

"Look!" he cried, spilling buttons and snow onto the freshly scrubbed table. "Mr. Ward gave them to me for my jacket."

His mother gasped.

"Run after him and give them back!" said his grandmother. "Buttons like that cost a small fortune."

"But I can't," said Jamie. "He is long gone."

"We must return them," said his father.

But how? Charles Ward had left no address.

"We'll put them away for safekeeping. Maybe he'll stop by on his way back," he said.

Jamie protested, but the buttons were locked away.

Weeks passed. Then, one day, a letter arrived addressed to Jamie's father. He read it aloud after supper.

Dear Sir,

I feel sure you think the gift I gave your son was a mere impulsive gesture, soon regretted. I write to tell you I have no regrets.

The buttons were intended as a gift for my son, Charles, but he was killed in our fight for freedom. If you are true patriots, as I believe you are, let your son wear them in memory of mine.

I remain, Sir, your obedient servant,
Charles Ward

In the silence that followed, Jamie's mother brushed away a tear.

"I will sew them on tonight," she said softly.

"It will be an honor for Jamie to wear them," said Jamie's father.

And that is how Jamie came to have silver buttons on his homespun jacket.

The Corduroy Churn

By Beth Thompson

"Ma! Ma, come quickly!" Jonas McAfee called breathlessly as he raced into the cabin. "Pa's laying the last logs on the road. It's nearly finished!"

Mrs. McAfee and her daughter, Comfort, set aside the mounds of bread dough they were kneading. Wiping their flour-dusted hands on their aprons, they hurried outside.

Tom McAfee was unloading the last of the long, rough-hewn logs from his wagon and laying them in a neat row across the narrow dirt road in front of their cabin. A broad grin spread across his mud-streaked face when he saw his family.

"A hard task, but nearly done!" he said. "How about that, Comfort? Your ma has her very own corduroy road, right up to her doorway. No more wheels getting stuck in the mud during wet weather!"

"Pa, why do they call it a *corduroy* road?" asked Jonas. "It's made out of logs, not cloth."

"Oh, Jonas, look at your breeches!" Comfort said, laughing. "See the bumpy little rows? They're just like the rows of logs on the road."

Jonas studied his worn, brown breeches. Sure enough, the corduroy material did resemble the newly laid log road. The road stretched before them like a long swatch of corduroy, leading from the McAfee cabin clear to Millstown, nearly ten miles away. Tom McAfee and three other farmers had laid the whole road, working off their tax debt and helping to make travel across Ohio easier for everyone. Jonas beamed proudly, because he'd helped cut and load the logs.

There were no hard-surfaced roads connecting towns in 1832. Most of the roads were no more than dirt tracks, swampy in the winter and dusty in the summer. Often the ruts in them were so deep a wagon would get stuck and have to be abandoned until teams of horses could come and pull it out. Then someone had the idea of putting logs across the dirt roads. The wagons bounced and jounced, but at least they got through.

"Pa, now that the wagon's empty, let's try out the new road," begged Comfort.

Pa was as eager as Comfort. "Only a short ride, though," he cautioned. "Brownie is mighty tired after hauling all this wood."

Ma agreed. "We'll have to get back soon to bake the bread," she said. "Comfort, go get that crock of cream for Granny Lewis. We'll ride past her cabin and leave it for her. Might as well combine errands with pleasure." Ma was never one to waste time or effort. It was a lesson the settlers learned quickly.

Comfort hurried to the little springhouse. Inside, it was dark and cool. The stoneware crock, full of cream, stood next to the big jar of milk it had been skimmed from.

Carefully cradling the crock in her arms, Comfort carried it to the wagon. She could hear the cream slosh as she set it down.

"Blackberry!" Jonas guessed.

"No, gooseberry. It was blackberry last time," Comfort insisted. Pa looked puzzled. Ma laughingly explained that they were guessing what kind of cobbler Granny Lewis might have made for them.

Every week the McAfees took fresh milk or cream or eggs to Granny Lewis. She wasn't their real grandmother, but Jonas and Comfort loved her just as much. In return for their kindness, Granny often made them a cobbler—a deep-dish dessert filled with juicy berries.

As the McAfee wagon rattled down the road, Comfort and Jonas were still guessing.

"Blackberry!"

"No, no, gooseberry! That's my favorite!"

During the ride the children bounced in the wagon like corn popping in a hot skillet. Comfort felt her teeth click together when the wagon hit a particularly rough patch. It was all she could do to keep the crock upright. Still, it was better than having to push the wagon out of ruts in the road.

Jonas shouted with excitement as he bounced. When the wagon pulled to a stop in front of Granny's cabin, he scrambled out, calling, "Granny! We rode on corduroy!"

"What's all the commotion?" Granny Lewis asked as she hurried out her front door.

"Here's your cream, Granny," said Comfort. "We brought it here on the new road."

"Just in time, too," said Granny. "I have a gooseberry cobbler cooling on the window ledge."

"You see! Gooseberry!" whispered Comfort to Jonas.

"Some of this cream will be tasty on the cobbler," said Granny, lifting off the wooden lid. Then she laughed delightedly. "Come see, Comfort. You've brought me a surprise!"

Comfort peered curiously into the crock. "Oh, my!" she gasped. Golden lumps bobbed in what was left of the cream. It was butter! The ride on the bumpy road had churned the cream into butter!

"That's surely the first time butter was ever made on corduroy!" Pa said with a laugh. "Maybe we should name this Butter Churn Road!"

Stage Fright for Jeremy

By J. W. Reese

"I can't do it," said Jeremy. "I just can't do it."

"But, Jeremy, you must give your speech and present the maple syrup to General Washington. You must," said Mother.

"But even thinking about it, I get so nervous I get the shakes. My knees tremble, and—"

"Jeremy!" Mother's voice was firm. "You know you were chosen by all of our friends to deliver the syrup to General Washington because you are the only son of Captain Gillet, Maple Hill's highest ranking officer killed in the Revolution."

"I know." Jeremy slumped into a chair and gazed at the floor. "I promised to give the syrup as a gift from all our neighbors. But, Mother, when we arrived here in New York City and I saw all these people, I got scared."

Mother twisted her hands. "You have your speech all memorized, do you not?"

"Of course. I could say it in my sleep," said Jeremy.

"Then just give the syrup to our new president, recite your speech, and it will all be over. If you can say it in your sleep, you won't forget it that easily."

"No, I know how it goes," said Jeremy. He rose to his feet and stood tall. "Mr. President, sir, on behalf of all the patriots of Maple Hill, West Stockbridge, Massachusetts, I—" He paused. "No, Mother, that's not the problem."

A knock sounded. Mother opened the door and welcomed a man with a round, red face and kind eyes. "Mr. Van Dong! Come in!"

Mr. Van Dong noticed Jeremy's unhappiness at once. "Young Gillet, why are you so sorrowful? Should you not be full of joy at seeing our new president tomorrow?" he asked.

"Jeremy does not feel he can deliver the speech tomorrow," said Mother.

"Why? Are you sick?" He placed his hand on

Jeremy's forehead. "I do not feel any fever." He turned to Jeremy's mother. "Is it that the food here in New York does not agree? I came to invite you both downstairs for supper, but perhaps it is better I tell Frau Van Dong to make some good hot broth instead." He turned to the door.

"No, it's not that." Mother sighed. "Tell him, Jeremy."

Jeremy was reluctant to talk. He kept his head down and said, finally, in a low voice, "I'm just afraid of all the people here."

"Ah!" Mr. Van Dong said softly. "Full of fear, is it?" He stared at Jeremy. "Afraid of all the eyes on you?"

"Yes, sir."

"Afraid you will forget what it is you are to say?"

"No, sir. I can remember that all right," said Jeremy. "But my knees get weak even thinking about it, and I am afraid I may even—" He swallowed and then continued, "—may even drop the jug of maple syrup at the general's feet."

"Ah!" Mr. Van Dong sat down. "And how shall we help you, Master Jeremy, to feel more able to do what you must?"

Jeremy felt a small sense of relief. This great Dutch merchant, in whose home they were staying, could surely think of something.

"You could, of course, send the jug and a note by a messenger," said Mr. Van Dong. "But that would not satisfy your friends who sent you here. They could have done that themselves. Or, you could have someone else hand the new president the jug while you recite the speech," he continued. "But that would not satisfy the wobbly knees, the pale face, the moist hands, no?"

"No," said Jeremy.

Again the Dutchman was silent. Then came a loud "Ah!" Mr. Van Dong rose to his feet. "Much of fear is a sense of the unknown. Perhaps if Jeremy could see the great general beforehand, say at the inauguration itself, he would not be so frightened afterward, eh?"

Jeremy could do no more than nod, though secretly he doubted even this would help.

"Space is very hard to obtain in the Federal Building. Only a few New Yorkers have seats. Even I must stand. But perhaps a small boy—" He faced Jeremy's mother. "I could take Jeremy with me and squeeze him in. I have a little influence here. Then, after the president's address, we could return to the president's house on Cherry Street in time to greet Mr. Washington after his visit to St. Paul's Chapel."

Mr. Van Dong walked to the door. "Come, Mrs. and Master Gillet. Let us partake of Frau Van Dong's fine cooking and then get a good night's rest for tomorrow. April 30, 1789, will be a day we shall all remember, eh?"

The next day the Senate Chamber was crowded, but as Mr. Van Dong had said, there was room for one small boy. Jeremy stood where he could clearly see the proceedings.

He looked over the newly-decorated chamber, the solemn senators and congressmen dressed in their finest, and the great crowd of standing spectators. His gaze was carried to the ceiling, upon which were painted a sun and thirteen stars. Ahead of Jeremy were three windows. Beneath the middle window was a small platform with three empty chairs.

The silence, the solemn men, the air of ceremony and formality all made Jeremy more aware of the enormity of what he must yet do. His fears returned in full force. But the heavy hand of the kind Dutchman resting upon his shoulder reassured him.

After a long wait amid whispers and muted coughs, the great moment came. Jeremy hardly noticed the formal proceedings as he waited for the entrance of the greatest man in the world—the man who would become the first president of the United States.

Soon, he came into the room. Jeremy took in every detail of the president's plain brown suit with silver buckles and buttons, white silk stockings, and silver-buckled shoes.

As the president seated himself on the podium, Jeremy gazed at Mr. Washington's face. The president was very pale and visibly trembling. "What's wrong?" Jeremy wondered. "The general must be ill."

Jeremy half-turned to whisper to Mr. Van Dong, but the president now arose and began his inaugural address. The great man was agitated and he trembled more than once. Several times he lost his place on the paper he was reading and seemed to have no idea of what to do with his hands.

"Could it be?" wondered Jeremy. "Could it be that our president is scared and nervous, too, after all he has been through during the Revolution?"

As General Washington continued, Jeremy was certain of it.

Why, if the greatest man in the world could do what he had to do in spite of the way he felt, then Jeremy could certainly do the same. He need not ever be afraid again.

Egg Day

By Peg Tyndal Jackson

Florence opened her eyes in the cold bedroom. She could see her breath in the pale morning light. Her first waking thought was, "Oh no! It's Egg Day!"

She burrowed down under the blankets with only her nose poking out. But a minute later she leaped out of bed and grabbed her red wool dress and underwear off the chair. She fumbled around for her shoes and stockings. Then she ran downstairs and plunked her clothes in front of the warm cookstove in the kitchen.

Mother Myers was slicing bread for the four children's lunches.

"It's Egg Day," Florence mumbled. "Mother, I don't believe I feel very good. Couldn't Daddy deliver the eggs?"

"Now, Florence," Mother said firmly, "you're perfectly well, and when you take the cutter to school we have no other transportation. Anyhow, Daddy has to work in the barn today." She spread some homemade peanut butter on a slice of bread.

"There's no reason in the world you can't deliver one crate of eggs to John Beck's store on your way home from school," she said.

"But, Mother," Florence's eyes pleaded, "what if some of the kids see me deliver the eggs?"

"Well, what if they do?" Mrs. Myers dished up a big bowl of oatmeal that had been cooking slowly all night. She set out some cream and brown sugar, and Florence, now washed and dressed, sat down at the table.

Florence swallowed hard. The oatmeal seemed lumpy today. "Do you know that the town kids laugh at us farm kids and call us hicks?"

Mother picked up a big, floppy bow and tied back Florence's dark, shining hair with it. She gave her daughter a hug. "I'll bet those children wish they could drive a horse to school every day. I'll bet they envy you!" she said.

Florence didn't look convinced. She finished her

breakfast and pulled on her black plush coat. She wrapped a long, woolly scarf around her head and grabbed her mittens. Mother handed Florence her lunch bucket. Then Mrs. Myers sat down to write a note to Florence's teacher.

"Don't tell her *why,* Mother! Just ask if I may be excused half an hour early. Maybe I can get the eggs delivered before the kids get out of school," said Florence.

"Fifteen minutes is early enough," Mother said. "The boys at the livery stable can have Colonel all hitched up and ready to go if you tell them you'll be there at a quarter to four."

Since Florence was the only child in the family going into town to school, it was her responsibility to hitch up old Colonel to the cutter. As she left the house, it was only 7:30 a.m. on a cold January morning in 1913.

Colonel was eating hay from his manger. Frosty air puffed from his nostrils. Florence got a bridle and harness down off the hook at the end of his stall. Since she was so much shorter than the horse, she threw the bridle over the top of his head. The bit on the bridle was icy cold, so she blew on it and warmed it in her hands.

As Florence opened Colonel's soft lips, she spoke to him. "Don't want to freeze your tender little mouth, old boy." Colonel accepted the clunky thing between his teeth.

When all the straps were fastened, she led him to the cutter out in the turnaround. Like a giant sled, it had runners. It was used over snow in winter, just as a buggy with wheels traveled summer roads.

Harnessing such a huge animal was a complicated process for a young girl. But Florence could do it, winter or summer, in about fifteen minutes.

Soon she was in the cutter, reins in hand, with a robe over her lap. She took a quick glance around her, hoping Daddy had forgotten to put in the crate of eggs. But there it was. "Oh well," she sighed, flicking the reins. "Off we go!"

The sun was now shining on a snowy wonderland of white trees. Particles of snow drifted lazily from the branches as the cutter moved down the snow-packed road. The air was clear and crisp and made Florence's nose tickle.

When she had driven the three and a half miles to town, she headed for the livery stable, only a block from school.

She drove up to a platform that was the same height as the floor of the cutter, so it was easy for her to step out. Inside the barnlike building, Colonel would be warm and dry and have hay and water whenever he wished.

"Good morning, Joe," Florence called to the stableboy who came to help her. "Colonel's oats for his lunch are here somewhere. And be sure to have everything ready by a quarter to four."

All day at school, Florence dreaded making her egg delivery. Shortly before four o'clock, she was back at the stable. Instead of going down Main Street to John Beck's store, she decided she would guide Colonel down the alley to the back entrance. That way, if any children from school came by, they wouldn't be able to see her.

The snow on Main Street was well packed and smooth from the runners of many sleighs. But in the alley there were rough places and icy spots. Suddenly, right in the middle of an icy patch, Colonel lost his footing and crashed to the ground.

The horse panicked and tried to scramble to his feet. But the ice was too slippery. His frightened neighs terrified Florence. She was sure from the way he was thrashing about that he'd break a leg.

Florence thought she could get hold of Colonel's head and calm him. While she was trying to grab his head, several boys and girls, now out of school, were attracted by the frantic sounds of the horse. They ran to Florence, and one of the biggest boys, Jim Lake, seemed to know just what to do.

Jim got Colonel to lie quietly on his side and motioned for Florence to hold the horse's head down on the ground. He reached into the cutter for the lap robe.

Florence kneeled by Colonel's head and stroked it. "Lovey Baby," she whispered, "you're going to be all right. Lie still. We'll have you up in no time."

Jim asked one of the girls to get more blankets from John Beck's store. He directed several boys to help him shove the blankets from the store under Colonel's back legs as the horse lay on his side.

"Now!" called Jim. They lifted Colonel's head, urging him to sit up. The horse tried to help. He turned the front of his body so that his front legs were on the blanket. He rose on his forelegs and shifted his hind legs around to give them footing on the back blankets. With a great lurch of his body, he rose on four feet. Everyone cheered.

Mr. Beck came out of his store and took the crate of eggs, having missed all the excitement.

"May we ride with you to the edge of town?" Helen Thompson asked Florence as soon as Colonel was hitched up again.

Billy Taber looked longingly at Colonel and said, "You're lucky to have a horse to drive to school!"

That night Florence said to her Mother, "Mama, they really seemed to like me! They thought I was lucky to live on a farm and have a horse to take me back and forth to school. They wished they were me! Can you believe it?"

Mother Myers looked at her young, brown-haired daughter, whose dark eyes glowed with happiness. "I believe it," she said, hugging Florence. "I really do believe it."

The Patchwork Stage Line

By Beth Thompson

The flat Texas prairie was so dry Maggie could see the hazy dust cloud thrown up by the horses' hoofs before she heard the rumble of the coach wheels and the familiar squeak-and-jingle of the team's harness. She raced from the barn to watch the stagecoach shudder to a stop. It was exciting to hear the driver's deep voice boom out over the noise of the coach, "Stage in! Whoa up! Whoa!" as he eased the tired and sweating horses to a standstill.

Maggie's parents managed one of the stations along the route of the Memphis to San Francisco stage line. The coaches came by twice each week and carried as many as a dozen passengers, but the mail pouches were the cargo most eagerly awaited by settlers along the route. There was no transcontinental railroad in 1860, and the frontier settlers depended on the overland stage and the Pony Express to bring news from friends and relatives back East.

Wright Station, where Maggie lived, was a "home station," where the coaches changed teams and the passengers, exhausted by hours of rough travel, climbed out to rest and enjoy a hot meal prepared by Maggie and her mother.

Jeremiah Stubbins was the driver Maggie liked best. His bristly beard looked fierce, but he always had a grin and time to chat with Maggie. Except for her baby sister, Maggie was the only child at Wright Station. She was often lonely. So when Mr. Stubbins visited the station it was a highlight in her life.

The stage often brought letters from Maggie's grandmother back in St. Louis. Maggie was particularly eager to see Mr. Stubbins today, as she had a letter to send to Grandma Taylor.

Maggie knew that her mother was often homesick for St. Louis, and so she wanted to make her a special birthday gift to remind her of home. She remembered the beautiful quilts on Grandma Taylor's beds, each square containing a colorful eight-pointed Missouri Star. So, she had written to her grandmother, asking for the pattern and some calico scraps to make a quilt for her mother. Maggie knew that Ma would be delighted to see the familiar quilt design.

She waited until the passengers had entered the station dining room before telling Mr. Stubbins her plan. He stopped unloading mailbags, and his face broke into a grin as she described the surprise.

"Your ma will be plumb tickled, Maggie. You can depend on Jeremiah T. Stubbins to do his part."

Weeks passed, and many coaches stopped at Wright Station, but there was no sign of Mr. Stubbins. Maggie worked on the simple patchwork squares that would form the quilt's border. But she knew she wouldn't have enough calico to finish the quilt. She began to worry. Even if the scraps and pattern arrived soon, could she possibly finish all the squares she'd need in time for her mother's birthday?

Every day Maggie watched for Mr. Stubbins's arrival. Then one morning she heard the familiar cry, "Stage in!" The coach creaked to a stop, and the weary passengers climbed out. Mr. Stubbins started handing down satchels.

"Something for you, too, Maggie!" he called. With a wink, he handed her one large bundle—and one of eight smaller packages! Maggie was mystified. What could they be?

The large bundle was from Grandma Taylor. It contained heaps of calico scraps in every color, a dozen completed squares, and the pattern for the Missouri Star. There was also a note:

Maggie dear,
  Good luck, and remember to keep your stitches small and even.

Love,
Grandma

Maggie smiled at the note. Then she turned to her friend. "Mr. Stubbins, what's in all the little packages?"

Jeremiah T. Stubbins blushed under his coating of Texas dust. "Well, I . . . I talked to some of the ladies at the other home stations about your surprise. They thought it was mighty fine that a little 'un like you was doing something special for her ma, and they wanted to help out in case you ran short of time. So, well, take a look!" He grinned and opened one of the packages. It contained six beautiful quilt squares and a note, saying:

This is the Delectable Mountain pattern. Hope these squares will be of use.

Lucinda Mooney
El Paso Station

Each package contained five or six quilt squares in a rainbow of colors, from states and stations all along the stage line. Maggie recognized some of the patterns: the tiny triangles of the Pine Tree, the patchwork circle called Sunburst, and the interlocking Wedding Rings. Others were new to her. And all of them were beautiful.

Maggie's eyes filled with tears at the thoughtfulness of these frontier women, taking time from their chores to help a little girl they didn't even know. "Ma won't believe it! The quilt will be a regular map of the stage line. A blanket of friends. Mr. Stubbins, if I hurry and write thank-you letters, would you deliver them for me?"

"I'd be pleased to," said Mr. Stubbins. He winked again. "Now, how about a plate of stew and a dozen or so hot biscuits? Keeping secrets makes a man mighty hungry!"

Maggie laughed and led the stage driver into the dining room to join the others.

The Secret of the Missing Pewter Plates

By Ann Bixby Herold

Jack Moon loved to swim. In England, where he was born, he swam in the river near his home. He could hold his breath underwater longer than anyone. He was still the neighborhood champion when the Moon family left for the New World.

The journey to America on a sailing ship was long and dangerous. There was a fearful storm, and a sailor was swept overboard. When they finally reached land, Jack's mother said that she would never set foot on a boat again.

At first Jack and his parents lived in Philadelphia. They had never lived in a town before. There was plenty to see, but Jack was lonely. It was hard to make friends in such a busy place. He spent most of his time on the waterfront, watching the sailing ships come and go. He listened to the sailors singing their sea chanteys. When a ship set sail for England, his heart ached.

"I miss my friends," he thought. "I wish I could go, too."

Jack's father soon found work with William Penn, governor of Pennsylvania. They were to live on his new plantation, Pennsbury Manor, and the only way to transport their possessions was by boat up the Delaware River. The water stayed calm during the journey, but Jack's mother worried all the way.

Pennsbury Manor reminded Jack of the big country mansions in England. It made him more homesick than ever, and the other boys on the plantation teased him about his accent. A big boy called Sam Taylor was the worst.

Everyone on the plantation had work to do. William Penn and his wife were coming soon on a tour of inspection.

One morning a barge arrived, loaded down with household goods. Jack wanted to help unload it, but Sam's father was in charge and Sam was with him, so Jack stayed away. He didn't hear about the missing pewter plates until later.

"The barge master swears the crate of pewter was aboard when they left Philadelphia," Jack's father said. "Yet it wasn't among the goods unloaded on this end."

"Was it stolen?" his mother asked. "Young Sam said he saw Indians nearby."

"Governor Penn thinks highly of our Indian neighbors, Molly," Jack's father said. "He won't like it if they are unjustly accused."

That night, while delivering a late message, Jack saw shadowy figures down by the landing. Sam Taylor was there, holding a lantern. Sam's friends, Henry and Roger, were with him. What were they doing there at that hour?

The next day the plantation was in an uproar. The missing crate contained not everyday pewter, as was first thought, but special plates given to the governor as a wedding gift. Everyone took part in a search. Jack was paired with Sam Taylor, and to his surprise, Sam ignored him. He looked worried. He seemed to search halfheartedly.

The crate was not found.

Late that night, on an impulse, Jack stole down to the landing. Sure enough, the three boys were there again. Sam was soaking wet. Jack moved closer and listened.

"Why didn't you tell your father?" Roger asked Sam.

"Because I didn't want to get into trouble. You dive now."

"I can't."

"*Please,* Roger." Sam sounded desperate. "The governor will be here tomorrow. I must get it out tonight, so it will be found by morning. if my father finds it on the landing, he will think the thief returned it."

"I can't swim underwater." said Roger.

"You try, Henry."

"I can't swim at all." said Henry.

"What will I do?" Sam groaned. "I can't hold my breath long enough to tie a rope around it."

"So that's what happened to the crate!" Jack thought. "Sam must have dropped it overboard."

He stepped out of the shadows. "I'll do it," he said.

"*You?*" Sam stared in disbelief.

As Jack stripped off his clothes, he stared into the pitch black water. It was making ugly sucking sounds against the pier. But Jack was a good swimmer.

"Give me the rope," he said.

Jack had to grope underwater in total darkness. Three times he came up for air. But at last the rope was secure, and the boys hauled the crate out of the water. Sam's whispered thank-you warmed Jack as he ran home in the chilly night air.

The crate was unpacked by the time the Penns arrived the next day. No one but the four boys ever knew it had been at the bottom of the river.

That's because the boys became friends. Everyone knows that friends are good at keeping secrets.

Nothing Stops Paul Revere

By Marcella Fisher Anderson

Rachel's voice rose up the stairway. "Why can't a younger man carry this message in the dead of night? You have seven children, Paul Revere."

"Yes, and it is for them I ride."

Sara sat up in bed. Quietly, she crept to the stairs. Under the railing she watched her father and stepmother in the cold light of the rising April moon.

"I can't understand why you're always the one sent. Ride to New York, ride to Philadelphia, and now tonight, ride to Lexington."

"Maybe I'm the best rider the patriots have." Sara's father chuckled and ran his finger down his wife's cheek.

Sara drew back. Rachel Walker had been her stepmother for only a year and a half. Sara was twelve now, in this year of 1775, and remembered her own mother very well. She remembered her father making that very same gesture to her. Sara tried to swallow the sudden tightness in her throat. She started quietly back up the stairs.

"Be careful then, Paul," Rachel said gently.

Sara leaned forward again. Just in time she saw the door quietly closing and their dog's tail disappearing through the narrowing opening. Sara could not help herself. "Rachel!" she whispered. "Dog went out, too."

Rachel spun around. "What—Sara?"

"The dog."

Rachel glanced at Dog's sleeping place by the hearth. "Oh, dear. Yes, well . . . he'll be back by morning. I can't risk opening the door again. It's nearly bright as day out there and time for the British night patrols to be out. You might as well come down," she went on briskly. "We'll have a cup of herb tea. There's a blanket by the fire."

As Sara lifted the steaming mug, she watched Rachel. Rachel was different from her own mother. More spirited perhaps. Sara set down her mug and smiled. Her own mother would never have stood up to her father that way. Still, Sara's heart ached when she thought of her. Would it never stop aching?

While Rachel was up in the bedroom tending to the crying of Baby Joshua, Sara heard a scratch-scratch at the door. What could it be? Dare she open the door when Rachel had already cautioned her against it? Scratch-scratch.

Carefully, Sara slid the bolt. With a chill blast of air, Dog ran in and sat down panting at Sara's feet. A rolled piece of paper hung from his collar. Sara untied it just as Rachel came down the stairs.

"Read it, Sara."

Sara unrolled the note. She read it aloud. "*'Tie my spurs to Dog's collar and send him back to me.'* . . . Father's spurs!"

"Get them quickly, Sara."

Sara tripped twice over the corner of her blanket as she hurried to the back room. Her father's spurs hung from a wall peg and shone in the moonlight.

Rachel pulled the narrow sash from her robe and handed it to Sara. "Tie them now. Hurry. Can you imagine? Forgetting his spurs!"

Sara's fingers were all thumbs. At last she made a final knot. She scooted Dog to the door and opened it quietly.

Two men were walking down the street. Sara knew they were Tories. She dared not make the noise of the latch clicking, so she held the door open barely a crack and waited.

"What fools these colonists are," Sara could hear through the door, "thinking they can fight the king's finest troops. Tomorrow may be their chance to find out what they're up against."

The voices faded. Sara wondered where the British patrols were tonight. What did the men mean about tomorrow? She held her breath and opened the door again. The street was empty. Then she slapped Dog on his hindquarters. "Now go," she whispered urgently. "Go back to Father."

Through the crack Sara watched Dog as he ran out to the street. Tail waving, he turned in the direction of the Charles River. With her heart still pounding, Sara went over to the fire. She poked the embers and sat with the blanket around her. She had no thought of sleep now and she knew that Rachel would stay awake, also. Still, as the hours passed, she slept fitfully, waking at last to the sound of Rachel crying softly.

Sara did not know how to comfort her. She left her place by the fire and walked over to the small window. It was nearly morning. In the early light she saw the apple trees in bloom, the grass greening in the yards. "I see it now," she thought aloud.

"What do you see?" asked Rachel, wiping her cheek. "The dawn?"

"I see that you love him, too."

Rachel crossed the floor so quietly that Sara hardly heard her until she stood behind Sara. "He is a joy of my life, as you are a joy of his, Sara."

Sara felt hot tears on her own cheeks. Then she turned to Rachel, who held her close.

A scratching sound came at the door. Sara rushed to open it.

Dog bounded into the room. His collar was empty.

Rachel clasped her hands. "Thank goodness," she said. "Once he is on horseback, nothing will stop Paul Revere."

● ●

The story of the forgotten spurs is true. In later years Paul Revere often told it to his grandchildren.

The Lunch Box

By Marilyn Kratz

"I'm ready, Grandpa," said Peter, but he didn't move from the washstand.

Grandpa put his hands on Peter's shoulders. "Your ma and pa often talked about this day—your first day of school," he said. "They wanted you to be an educated man, maybe a lawyer or a doctor."

Peter looked down. "I would rather stay home and learn to be a farmer like you."

Grandpa sighed. "I'm not much of an example for you, lad."

"It's not your fault," Peter spoke up quickly. "We just happened to settle here in dry times. You're a good farmer—a good carver, too."

"Carving is only for pleasure," said Grandpa, looking out the door of the small sod house at the parched prairie beyond. "If we don't get a better crop next year, we won't make it through the winter. It'll be hard enough this year."

"I could get a job in the settlement instead of going to school," said Peter.

"Now, I don't want to hear such nonsense," said Grandpa. He went to the cupboard and took something out of it. "I made this for you."

Peter gasped. "Grandpa! It's beautiful!"

Grandpa had carved Peter a lunch box that looked like a train engine. Every detail was perfect, from the cowcatcher at the front to the engineer's cabin at the rear. The wheels even turned.

"There's honey bread inside," said Grandpa, grinning at the surprised look on Peter's face.

"It's wonderful, Grandpa. Thank you," said Peter.

"Well, it won't do to be tardy the first day," said Grandpa. And, for the first time, he extended his hand to Peter instead of giving him a hug and kiss. "Have a good day, Peter."

Peter felt his stomach tighten as he shook Grandpa's hand. Then he took a deep breath and left.

As Peter walked toward the settlement, he tried to think of excuses to turn back. He began to worry.

Would there be a desk for him? Would the bigger boys laugh at the patches on his pants?

Peter's steps slowed as he approached the schoolhouse, and he stopped to watch the children play.

A boy about his size ran up to him. "Want to play 'pump-pump-pull-away' with us?" he asked.

Peter just stood there, wishing his feet didn't feel so heavy. The boy looked at him for a moment, then rejoined the game. Peter was relieved to hear the school bell ring. He went in with the others.

The children placed their lunches on a shelf along the back wall. Most of the children had brought their lunches in shiny tin pails. A few had theirs tied in cloths. Not one had a carved lunch box like Peter's. Suddenly, Peter felt embarrassed about his. He slid it way back on the shelf where it wouldn't show.

The teacher rapped on her desk with a ruler.

"Good morning, boys and girls," she said. "I'm Miss Swenson. Our first task will be to plan our seating arrangement. All who are in the third reader, please sit at the back of the room."

Most of the big boys and girls moved back, two children sharing each desk. Miss Swenson seated those in the second reader in front of them.

"Now, those in the beginning reader will sit up front," said Miss Swenson.

The smaller children scrambled to find seats. Then only Peter was left standing.

"What reader are you in?" asked Miss Swenson.

"I don't have a reader," Peter said. He felt his ears turn red.

"You may use this one," said Miss Swenson, handing him a beginning reader. "There's one seat left at the front." She indicated a desk already occupied by a little girl. "You may share that desk with Molly."

Peter heard some snickers as he took his seat. He didn't return Molly's friendly smile.

Peter listened carefully as Miss Swenson assigned the lesson. He copied the letters as she wrote them, and he quickly learned their names and sounds.

"Very good, Peter," said Miss Swenson. "You'll soon be in the second reader."

Peter glanced back. Jonathan, the boy who had invited him to play, grinned at him. Peter hoped he would be able to share a desk with him soon.

The morning passed quickly. Then Miss Swenson announced, "Lunchtime."

Suddenly, Peter felt embarrassed again as he remembered his beautifully carved lunch box.

"Want to sit together to eat lunch?" Jonathan asked.

Peter hesitated. Then he followed Jonathan to his desk, carrying his fancy lunch box under his arm. As soon as he set it on Jonathan's desk, his new friend exclaimed, "What's that?"

"My lunch box," Peter said. He hunched down in the seat, afraid that Jonathan would make fun of it.

"Where did you get it?" asked Jonathan.

"My grandpa made it."

"It's really nice!" said Jonathan. "May I touch it?"

"Yes," said Peter, wishing Jonathan wouldn't talk so loudly.

"Bob!" Jonathan called to his older brother. "Come look at this."

Several big boys crowded around Jonathan's desk. Peter wished more than ever that he had stayed home.

"Do the wheels really turn?" asked Bob.

"Has your grandpa made any others?" asked another boy.

"Would he make one for me?" asked another.

Miss Swenson came to see what was causing all the excitement. She examined the carved lunch box.

"Your grandfather is a talented carver," she said. "Do you think he would like to make some for my father to sell in his general store?"

"I don't know," Peter said, trying to think. He knew Grandpa loved to carve. Now that the harvest was in, he had spare time. And the extra money would help get them through the winter. "I'll ask him," Peter said.

When the others returned to their desks, Jonathan said, "I would like to meet your grandpa sometime."

Peter grinned as he took the honey bread from his lunch box. "I'm going to be just like him," he said. "And he's going to be proud of me when I tell him that I like going to school."

The Hobo

By Emma L. Hickman

The day the hobo came was a warm and beautiful spring morning in 1933. Meg was perched on her favorite limb in the apple tree. She heard the freight train whistle. From where she sat she could see a hobo coming down the dusty road with a small pack over his shoulder. He headed for Meg's house.

Meg's mama always fed the hoboes. Sometimes there were eight or ten lined up on the back porch. She piled their tin plates high with biscuits and gravy, sausage, and eggs. She gave them steaming cups of black coffee.

This morning there was only one hobo. Meg watched from her perch as he ate slowly, without bolting his food.

While he was finishing his coffee, Mama went to the shed and brought back an ax and a saw. The hobo stretched and took the tools from Mama.

He was coming toward the orchard!

Meg tried to hide behind the apple blossoms, but he walked right up to her.

"You must be Meg," He said. "Your mama told me I'd find a freckled monkey climbing an apple tree in the orchard." His smile lit up his whole face. "I'm Will. I'm here to chop down the dead apple tree." He held out the largest hand Meg had ever seen.

Meg carefully shook his hand. "Where are you from?" she asked.

"I travel all over the country on the trains," he said. "When I find work, I stop awhile."

"Don't you have a home?" she queried. She was instantly sorry she had asked, because she saw a shadow cross his face.

"I had a home once, and a loving wife and a little daughter about your age," he said. "They died a few years ago. That's when I took to the trains."

Meg's papa hired Will to stay and help with extra work. He ate his meals with the family but insisted on sleeping in the barn. Papa said that Will was a mighty good worker.

Meg began spending most of her Sundays and evenings with Will, listening as he told stories about the many postcards in his picture album. Sometimes they sat on the back porch, but most often they went to the orchard. Will sat in the tall grass with his back against the apple tree. Meg sat above him on her favorite limb. Each time, she picked a card from the album and Will told a story about it. He had postcards from everywhere.

Will described wildflowers growing in the open fields of Nebraska until Meg could smell the scent of the blossoms.

He recalled the green fields and flaming autumn hillsides in New England.

Will told her about a postcard of a lone shepherd tending his sheep on a Wyoming plateau.

He described California palms swaying in the moonlight, and sandy beaches covered with driftwood, and huge waves crashing on the shore. He imitated the cry of sea gulls. Meg almost wanted to cry herself at how lonesome the sea gulls sounded.

One morning the kitchen was buzzing with excitement when Meg went down to breakfast. It was time for their spring lambs to be born.

"Two of the ewes had twins," Papa was saying to Will. "They're each rejecting the second lamb. You and Meg can build a pen behind the wood stove for the lambs."

Meg's mama got busy washing bottles. Will gathered boards, and Meg carried nails. As they built the pen, Will explained that the warmth from the stove would keep the lambs comfortable.

When they were finished, they went to the sheep shed to gather the lambs. Meg's cheeks were pink with excitement as she carried her warm, woolly lamb and put him behind the stove.

"He thinks I'm his mother!" Meg laughed as the lamb nuzzled closer. "I'll call him Curly," she announced proudly.

Will deposited the other lamb in the pen. "My lamb looks sleepy," Will said. "I'll call him Nod." Will and Meg started for the door.

"You two stop right there!" Mama called. "These lambs need to be fed." She gave Will and Meg each a bottle of warm milk.

Will picked up his lamb and put the bottle in its mouth. He looked all arms and legs. With that big grin of his, he made Meg and Mama laugh.

Meg's lamb stepped all over her in his eagerness to eat, shaking his curly tail while the milk ran down his face.

"That little one eats like a pig!" Will exclaimed.

Meg laughed. "So does Nod," she countered.

Mama got her big box camera and took a picture of them. "For your album, Will," she announced.

Papa came in. They all sat on the back porch and enjoyed a glass of Mama's lemonade.

The lazy summer went by. Meg had never been so happy, but Mama and Papa began to look troubled. Sometimes they talked in hushed tones. Once Mama told Meg that things don't always stay the same. Sometimes, she said, it's necessary to make changes. Meg felt uneasy.

One Sunday Meg hurried down to breakfast, eager to hear one of Will's stories. But only Mama and Papa were at the table. Papa told Meg gently that there was no longer enough work for Will. He had taken his pack and left during the night.

Meg could hardly breathe for the sudden ache in her chest. Tears blinded her as she excused herself and ran for the orchard.

All the way to the orchard, she cried softly. "I hate him. I hate him! How could he leave without saying good-bye?" she thought. Didn't he know he had taken a piece of her heart?

Meg climbed into the apple tree. There, she saw the picture album placed neatly on her favorite limb. Tears streamed down her face as she hugged the album, then opened it. Inside, Will had written: *Take care of our album until we meet again. Forever your friend, Will.*

Meg smiled through her tears. The hobo had left behind a piece of his heart, too.

Secrets
of the
State House

By Elizabeth Van Steenwyk

James sat in the shade against the wall of the Pennsylvania State House, batting at flies and sweating. Folks said this summer of 1787 was the hottest they could remember.

If James hadn't wanted to see the general walk back and forth to his lodgings each day, he wouldn't have stayed much longer. It was too hot.

How he longed to talk to the general. George Washington was his hero, and James wanted to be just like him. It was said that General Washington was the bravest leader in the land. At least that's what Father told him, and he should know. Father had served with him in the war, when the colonies had rebelled against British rule.

"James, are you here again today?"

James looked up to see his best friend, Henry, leaning against the wall. "The men should be coming out soon, and then you can see him, Henry."

"The General, you mean?" said Henry. He scuffed up dust with his foot and squinted against the sun. "I saw him yesterday and the day before that."

"But today he might speak to us," said James.

"Oh, James, that's what you always say. He doesn't have time for us. He's always talking to those men."

James drew a line in the dirt with his fingers. That was true. The General was a busy man, thinking about the nation's business. Inside the hall they were writing something very important. Father called it a constitution.

"They must be hot in there with the windows and shutters closed," James said, wiping his forehead with his shirt sleeve.

"Why don't they open them?" Henry asked.

"Because they've taken a vow of secrecy," James whispered. "If the windows were open, others could learn their secrets."

"Is that a fact?" Henry sat down beside him. "Where

did you hear that?"

"Father read it in the *Gazette*. This constitution-thing is hard to write, I guess," said James.

Suddenly Henry sat up straight. "Say, maybe we can find out some of their secrets and tell the *Gazette* about them." He pressed an ear close to the wall. "Then we'll be heroes."

James leaned into the wall. "I can't make out the words, can you?"

Henry listened for a moment before he shook his head. "No," he said, "it's just a lot of mumbling to me." He stood up and stretched. "Come on, James. Let's go to the river and swim."

James was tempted to go. How many days had he waited for a chance to speak to the general? Why not give up? Swimming would be a lot more fun, and he'd feel much cooler. So why didn't he go?

"I'm going to wait a little while longer," he said

Henry shook his head. "The sun has gotten to you," he said. "It has made you feverish."

"Maybe so," James said. He leaned back against the wall of the building and watched Henry follow the curving path to the river.

Now he squinted against the brightness. Puffy white clouds sailed past the patch of sky he saw through nearby trees. Too bad they didn't dump some rain and cool the air.

James was startled when he heard a door slam inside the State House. The meeting was over. They would be coming out now. The general would walk right by him again if he didn't do something.

James scrambled to his feet and ran to the corner of the building. The ailing Ben Franklin was carried past on his stretcher. James Madison scampered by, small as a boy himself. Others walked in groups of twos and threes, talking, talking. They never seemed to stop talking.

The general would be among the last to leave. James knew that from days of watching. He sighed as he watched the last group of men walk past.

Then he saw a slip of paper fall out of someone's writing book. No one noticed it. The men kept walking as the paper landed to one side of the path.

Maybe that piece of paper contained something important. If James read it, he might know some of the secret goings-on inside the State House. He could take it to the *Gazette,* and it would be published. *Secrets of the State House, told by James Burney.*

But somehow that didn't sound right. Would a hero tell a secret that wasn't his to tell?

James ran to the paper and picked it up. It felt hot in his hands, but not from the sun. It blistered his fingers with temptation. What should he do? Read it and tell?

Then James knew. The general had been keeping the secrets of the State House since May. They were important to him, so they were important now to James. He knew that he couldn't look.

A shadow took shape on the path beside him. It was a shape so large he was startled by it. He glanced up.

"General," James blurted out, "I have something for you."

General Washington smiled down at him. He seemed as tall as an oak tree. "What might that be?"

"This fell from someone's writing book." James handed him the slip of paper. His hand trembled only a little.

The general frowned, and then he smiled at James. "Thank you. You have done a good thing today, young man. You have kept our secrets safe."

James nodded, unable to speak as he watched the general walk down the path. When the tall figure was a small one in the distance, James turned and raced toward the river, feeling sweaty and hot.

"Wait until I tell Henry about this," he thought. "I shared a secret with the general. A secret of the State House!"

Then he slowed down and nearly laughed out loud. Henry would never believe him. Never in a million years. "Might as well keep the whole secret," he thought. "It will be my secret alone, with the general."

Dust Storm

By Trish Collins

John lived on a small farm in the dust bowl, the dry and windy plains east of the Rocky Mountains. Alone on the farm, he pushed through the hot strong wind to the barn and went in.

His mare, Peggy, pounded her front hoofs on the plank flooring in greeting. She was born the same year as John, ten years ago. Together they had explored the dusty countryside under the hot summer sun, John always riding bareback, his bare feet tucked around Peggy's strong body.

This morning, before riding to town for supplies, his father had said, "Keep watch to the west for a dust storm. If the sand begins to drift and the air fills with dust, go down the road to Mrs. Emerson's farm. Neither of you should be alone during a storm."

The cows and sheep in the barn seemed restless, but they had plenty to eat and drink. They would be safe here in the barn. John wanted to be certain of that before he left. It was getting harder and harder to see. Day was becoming dark as night. Dust was cutting off the sun's rays. John didn't like the gritty dust he could taste in his mouth even here in the barn. Soon it would be difficult to breathe outside. John felt uneasy and uncertain of what he should do. "Go to Mrs. Emerson's," his father had told him. But would he and Peggy make it through the storm?

John looked out the small west window. He saw the sand swirling around in the strong wind. They had about five minutes before the greatest cloud of dust would whip over the farm. With the wind behind them, maybe he and Peggy could reach Mrs. Emerson's farm ahead of the thickest cloud.

He swallowed, fear rising in his dry throat. He ran to his horse and bridled her. "The dust will get in our lungs," he said to the mare. "What can I do to stop it? If we don't cover our noses, we might not be able to breathe out there."

Peggy backed out of her stall.

"A blanket!" John said. "A wet blanket! That would

help. There must be an old one around here."

In the corner he found a torn blanket. Taking it to the watering trough, he opened it up, and dropped it into the water.

When he pulled it out of the water, it was so heavy he could barely lift it. He tried to wring out some of the water, but that was impossible. He bunched the dripping blanket in his arms and hurried back to Peggy. Now they had something to catch the dust and cover them both.

"This wet blanket may feel cool," John said, putting it up on Peggy's back. He was right. Peggy pranced about to shake it off. "Peggy, we've got to have it. Steady, girl, steady."

John pushed against the barn door with all his strength and led Peggy out into the storm.

By now it was impossible to see more than a few yards ahead. Coarse sand bit against John's face. Wind swirled dust into his eyes.

John threw his body across the mare's back, almost losing the blanket over the side. Throwing his leg over, he pulled the blanket over his head and sat up. He pushed part of the blanket over Peggy's head. She jumped back, but under John's gentle urging, she finally pranced out to the road.

John found a hole in the old blanket for Peggy to see through. He shouted into their tent, "Giddap!"

Peggy galloped down the road to Mrs. Emerson's farm and stopped at the barn. John lifted the blanket.

The barn door was banging back and forth. He wondered why Mrs. Emerson had left it open with a storm coming up. He pulled the blanket off and slid to the ground.

He could now see only a few feet ahead. Suddenly John saw Mrs. Emerson lying on the ground by the door. "Mrs. Emerson, what's the matter?" he called.

John ran over and knelt down by her. She was coated with sand, and her face was pale. He lifted her head into his lap. She squinted up at him.

"Help me into the barn," she whispered.

John helped her sit up. Then he hooked the barn door open so it would not bang against them. With Mrs. Emerson leaning on John, the two inched their way to the barn through the dark, choking dust.

When they were inside and Mrs. Emerson was seated on a bench, John brought Peggy into the barn. After the horse was in, John unhooked the door. The wind tried to grab it, but John pulled hard and managed to latch it shut.

He sat down next to Mrs. Emerson. "Are you all right?" he asked. "What happened?"

"I'm all right now. But I'm glad you came," she said softly. "When the wind came up, I came out to close the barn door. The wind grabbed the door and me, and somehow I hit my head. The next thing I remember was your voice." She smiled. "Thank you."

The storm was raging outside, but John, Mrs. Emerson, and Peggy were safe.